The Mouse in the Manger

The Mouse in the Manger

Story by Rev. Gennaro L. Gentile

Art by Vernon McKissack

Ave Maria Press·Notre Dame, Indiana 46556

Special thanks to Jonathan Hall and Anne MacDonald for their help in preparing this manuscript.

© 1978 by Ave Maria Press, Notre Dame, Indiana 46556

Library of Congress Catalog Card Number: 78-72944
International Standard Book Number: 0-87793-165-8

Manufactured in the United States of America.

Foreword

The *Mouse in The Manger* is not only a delightful story with lovely visuals that can be enjoyed by children, but it is also useful to parents and teachers as a teaching tool.

Used creatively the story can form the basis of a parable in Christmas liturgical celebrations—either on the last school day before the Christmas recess or on Christmas Eve itself. For example, place an empty manger prominently in front of the altar and entrust a statue of the infant Jesus to a young child. As the children enter church, each is given a handful of straw. The story is read or acted out (perhaps with puppets), either before Mass or following the Liturgy of the Word. At an appropriate time, perhaps at the preparation of the gifts, the children are invited to come forward and place their straw in the empty manger. When they have done so, the young child steps forward and places the statue in the manger, on the donated straw, while an appropriate carol is sung.

In using the book in the classroom, the teacher can talk about the various characters and who and what they represent. For example Oscar, the mouse, is typical of a young boy or girl; Martha, the cow, is a snob and selfish; Hank, the sheep, follows the crowd, and Sidney, the Donkey, has been offended so he retreats into himself.

All children have a little of each character in them, and the ability to see their own actions in the actions of the characters will greatly enhance their participation in the story.

In Oscar's adventure he feels loneliness for the first time and discovers the meaning of a friendship and sharing. The call to discipleship and to service is the key to the tale. We are invited to give ourselves and to live in a different way once we encounter Christ. Nothing in our lives can ever be the same again.

A long, long time ago a family of mice lived in a burrow under a large grassy field. They had lived there for many years, and their home was very large and warm and comfortable. The entrance was in the field and when you came down the tunnel you came into a very large room. Each member of the family had his own bedroom. Each mouse had a straw bed.

The name of the youngest mouse was Oscar. Oscar loved his family, especially all his brothers and sisters, but for him the most special thing in the whole world was his straw bed. He used to play in the straw, crawl into it and curl up. Covered with straw, he would fall asleep.

But Oscar wanted a bigger bed. One day, he went to his father and said, "Dad, I'm getting bigger and I need more straw for a larger bed."

His father said to him, "Oscar, I would like to give you more straw, but we don't have any more. It is winter now and the snow is covering the grass. You will have to wait until spring. When it is warm again, I promise I will get you more straw."

Oscar was angry. He yelled at his father, "I want it now! I don't want to wait till springtime!!"

His father said to him, "Enough, Oscar. I have explained it to you. Don't yell at me! We will get the straw when the weather is warmer. Go to your room."

Oscar was now very angry. He went to his room. He held his head in his hands and said to himself, "I need more straw for my bed. If they really loved me they would give me the straw. My father is not fair in sending me to my room. I have every right to be angry! Since they do not love me, I will not stay here. I'll run away tonight. I'll miss my brothers and sisters, but I'll go anyway!"

That night, after everyone had gone to bed, Oscar very quietly tip-toed out of his room. He took his clothes and toothbrush and tied them to a short stick. Softly he walked through the living room and slipped out into the field. The only light came from one large star. The star gave off a blue-white light so Oscar could see where he was going. He was scared because he was leaving home. He was so cold and lonely, he almost went back. Then he thought of the straw. He said to himself, I am going to find straw for a nice big bed. With that he set off.

Oscar walked and walked and walked. He got colder and colder.

He came to the top of a hill and he could see sheep and some shepherds. They had built a little fire to warm themselves. Across from Oscar was another hill. In the side of the hill was a cave. Someone had built a stable in the cave. Oscar could see some animals. He was shivering from the cold. He said, "Maybe I can spend the night there. At least I could get out of the wind and cold."

So Oscar ran down the hill. He stopped at a road which ran down the middle of the hills. He looked both ways to see if anything was coming and then quickly went across the road, stopping at a sign. One arrow pointed to "Bread Town"; the other arrow pointed to "Peace City." That sounds like a nice place to visit. I must go there some day, he said to himself.

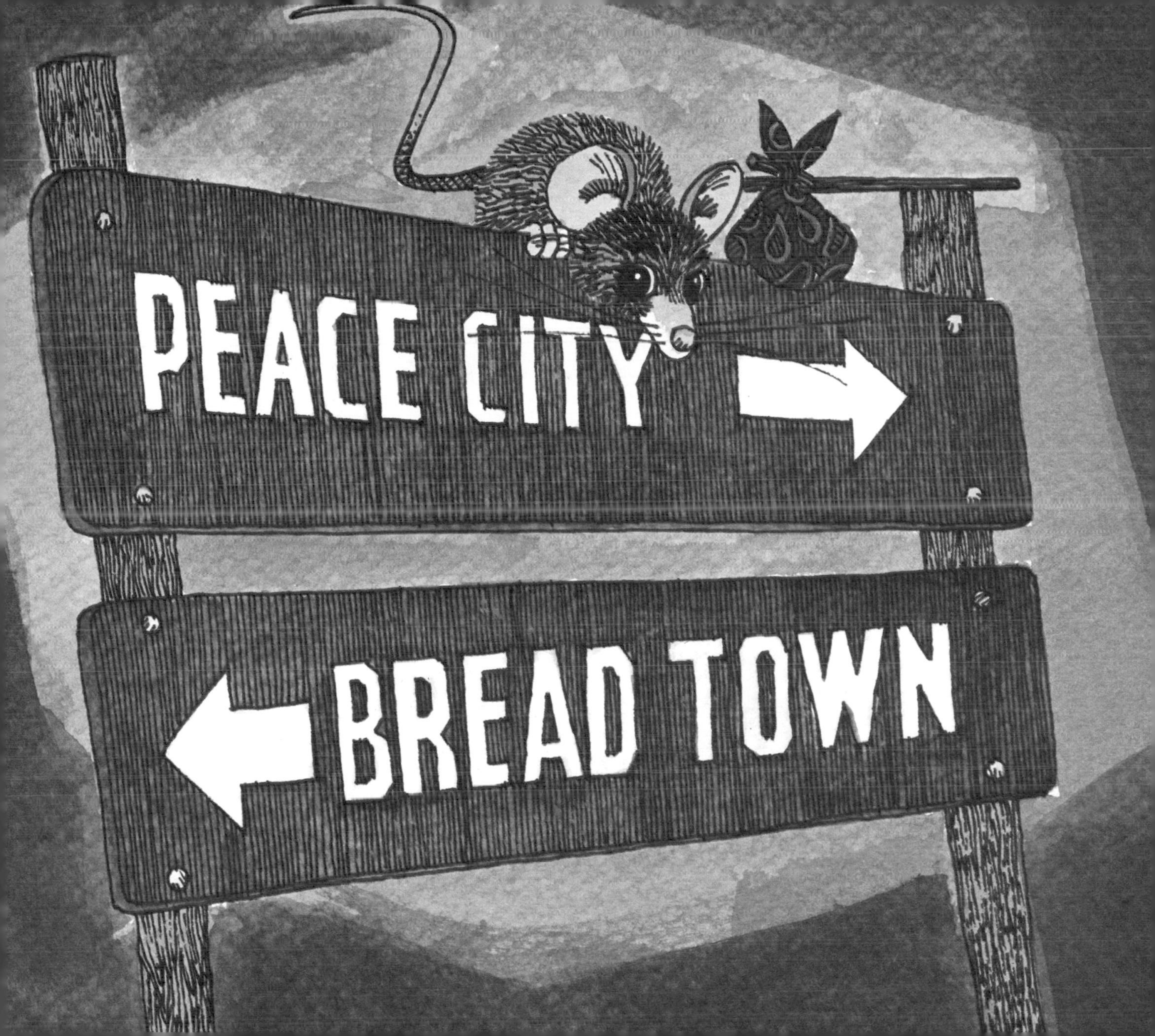
PEACE CITY
BREAD TOWN

He started climbing up the gray stones to get to the stable. Huffing and puffing he came up to a rock where he could get a good look at the stable.

The cave went back about 10 feet. The wind had eaten the rock out in a half circle. It wasn't very high. The tallest part was only about six feet. A four-foot wall made of medium size stones was all around it. A wooden gate, hooked together by a rope, kept the animals in. Wooden stalls inside kept the wind out. A cow, a few sheep and two donkeys were the only animals Oscar could see.

Oscar walked up the hill to try to get in. The spaces were too small for him to fit through. He peeked in through a space. Much to his delight, there was straw all over the floor. He ran to the front gate and pushed against one of the doors. The door slowly moved and then stopped. The latch, way up high, stopped the door. Too high for me to reach, thought Oscar. He tried again and a crack appeared between the doors. Too small for a cow or a sheep or a donkey but just right for a mouse. Quick as a wink, Oscar slipped between the gates.

The stable was much bigger than it looked from the outside. Oscar stood at the door, feeling warm for the first time since he had run away from home. He kept looking at the heaps and piles of straw. "Oh wow!" he said, and ran around picking up the straw.

Suddenly a huge shadow with horns covered him and a voice boomed, "What do you think you're doing with that straw?"

Oscar was very scared. He slowly turned around at the huge form which had him trapped. "I, I, I was just, just, picking up some loose straw. . ." he stammered.

"Who told you you could touch our straw?" demanded the voice. In a tiny, little voice Oscar squeaked,

"No one."

"What did you say?" thundered the voice.

"No one, sir" repeated Oscar, very frightened now.

"It's not 'sir'; my name is Martha. What is your name?"

"Oscar," he replied.

"Oscar? hmmm. . . we don't have any mice in this stable, but as the head cow I might let you stay. What can you do for us, Oscar?"

"Do? I never thought of that," replied Oscar.

"Well, you can't stay if you can't do anything. We have no room for a lazy mouse," said Martha.

"Wait, wait," cried Oscar. "I'm small, I can pick up things you drop or lose. I can crawl into tiny spaces for you; please let me stay."

Martha struck the ground with her brown hoof, "Well, we'll give you a try. You can stay." The brown and white cow turned away.

Oscar called after her, "Martha! May I please have some straw? I will put it into the corner and make a bed for myself."

Martha stopped and looked over her shoulder. "Just a little bit from my pile. If you want more, you'll have to ask the other animals."

"Thank you, Martha." said Oscar. "You're a real friend."

"Friend? I am not your friend, little mouse!" yelled Martha as she turned her huge body back to Oscar.

Frightened, he dropped his straw. "I thought you were my friend because you let me stay and said I could have the straw." The words poured out because Oscar was afraid that Martha was angry with him.

"Ha, ha, ha!" laughed Martha. "Friend! That's a joke. Cows can't be friends with mice. I am a very important cow. You are a tiny little mouse. My friends are only other cows. You are silly, Oscar, to expect a cow of my importance to be friends with a mouse!" With that, Martha gave a snort and, in a very dignified way, turned and waddled back to her stall.

Oscar was hurt. He wondered why mice and cows couldn't be friends. He picked up a piece or two of straw and walked to the back of the cave. He put the straw into a little pile and started back to get more.

Oscar was talking to himself, "I wonder why we couldn't be friends?"

"Friends?" a voice said, "Wah sure we can be friends."

Oscar jumped. "Who are you?"

"Mah name is Henry. Mah friends call me Hank. You can call me Hank. What's your problem, boy?"

"Well, I wanted to get out of the cold and get some straw for a bed and be a friend and Martha said no and. . ."

"Slow down, boy! Too many words! You want some straw—here take some. You want a friend, I'll be your friend." A big wide smile filled Oscar's face.

He was about to open his mouth when Hank said,
    "We can be friends next Tuesday afternoon. Yup, Tuesday morning I've got to eat, Tuesday night I said I'd be friends with Jessie. I can fit you in Tuesday afternoon. We'll be friends from after lunch until dinner. Yup." With that Hank walked away and started talking to the other sheep.

Oscar's big smile had vanished. Tears were filling his eyes. He bent down to pick up some straw. Slowly, so slowly, he carried them to add to his little pile. "A little more and I'll be done," he said to himself. So he got up and peeked into the stall next to Martha's.

"Excuse me, may I have some of your straw?"

A head with two giant ears opened and two little eyes stared right at him. "Who are you? What do you want from me?" was the angry question.

"My name is Oscar, sir. I am gathering straw together for my bed. I would like to be your friend."

The donkey stomped his foot. "Sidney's the name, Oscar. You help yourself to the straw." Oscar was surprised at the answer.

He said to Sidney, "Your voice doesn't sound friendly but you are giving the straw to me. Do you want to be my friend?"

Sidney turned his head away. Softly he said, "No."

Oscar asked "Why not?"

In a teeny voice, with his head still turned away, Sidney answered, "I want to be your friend. I want to have friends. But if I became your friend, I might accidently step on you someday. You are so little and I am so big. Then if I hurt you and we are friends I would feel bad. But if I don't know you or like you, then it doesn't matter what happens to you. If you get hurt, then I won't feel bad."

"But, but," Oscar cried out, "what about the good times? We could play together and have fun together."

"That only makes it worse," said Sidney. "The more I like you the more I risk getting hurt. No, friendship is dangerous business. Take the straw, little Oscar, and go." With that Sidney fell silent.

Oscar took the straw and finished his bed. He crawled into it. It was perfect. Much bigger than his bed at home. But he missed his brothers and sisters. He thought of his father and about the fight they had had. He fell asleep thinking about Martha, Hank and Sidney.

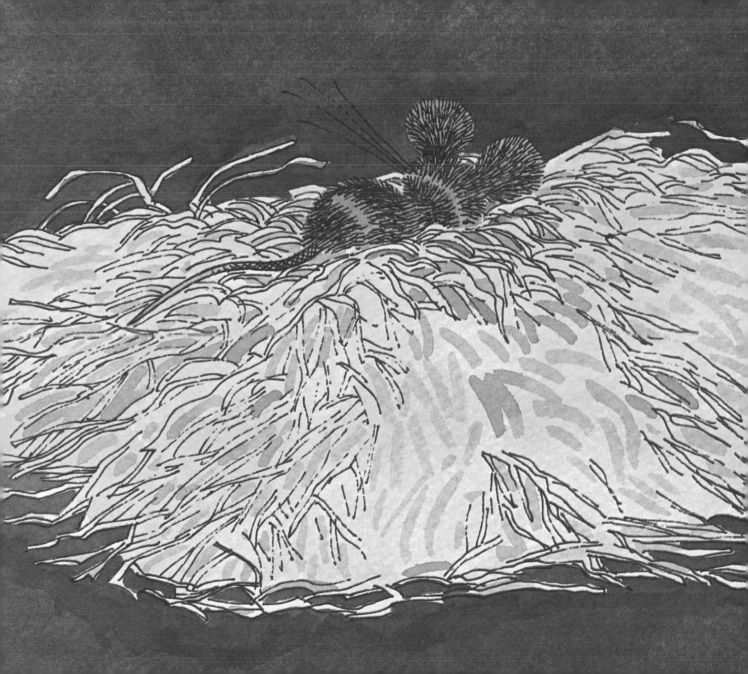

He was asleep for a short while when a loud noise woke him up. He opened his eyes and blinked a few times. The stable was flooded with light from the blue-white star. Oscar looked to see the cause of the sound. He saw two people standing at the gate. One was helping the other walk.

The smaller one, a woman, came in a few steps and laid down next to the rocky wall. She held her stomach. Her stomach was very big and stuck out. Every minute or two, her whole stomach would move. The lady would moan softly. She said something to the man, who quickly left.

Oscar slowly crept over to the woman. "Eek!" she screamed.

"Oh, don't be frightened," said Oscar, "What's your name?"

"My name is Mary," replied the lady. "And yours, little grey mouse?"

"My name is Oscar. I'm looking for a friend."

"Tell me, little Oscar, have you found a friend?"

"First, I met Martha. I couldn't be her friend because I wasn't important enough. She wanted me to be someone I'm not and could never be. She turned me down. She didn't want to be my friend!"

"There, there, now." Mary said in a soft voice. "That's Martha for you. A good friend leaves you free. He lets you be the best person you can be. There are no strings to real friendship. A friend is a mirror of yourself. He lets you see yourself as you are. He lets you be who you are right now."

"It all sounds so simple," Oscar squeaked.

"Oh, I'll tell you a secret. A friend gives you the power to become the best person you can be. You have the choice because a good friend gives you the freedom with this power."

"This power," Oscar asked, "does it have anything to do with something Hank said? He told me he could only be my friend on Tuesday afternoon. Can you turn this power on and off?"

"Oh, no, no, no!" There was a small smile on Mary's face. "Once you say to someone, 'I will be your friend,' then that person is special. A real friend isn't there only on Tuesday afternoons or until you become someone else. A friend is always there."

"I wanted to be Sidney's friend, but he said no. He told me he didn't want to get hurt."

"He's right, Oscar. To be a friend you have to leave yourself wide open. That's so the love in your heart can reach out to your friend and your friend can reach in to touch your heart."

"Oh, you could reach in and hurt your friend," said Oscar, his eyes wide open with wonder.

"Yes, Oscar, but that's the secret. The power of friendship is the risk you are taking with a friend. You are willing to be hurt so that your friend can be free to be whoever he wants to be. That's where the power comes from."

With that, Mary's stomach started to rise and fall and she grew short of breath. "My baby is coming. My baby boy is going to be born."

Eager to help, Oscar asked "Can I do anything?"

"Why, yes, my little friend. We have no bed to put the baby in. We will have to use the crib which holds the animals' food. Can you find some straw so that my baby can sleep comfortably?"

Oscar lowered his eyes. He wanted to help the lady, but he wanted his cozy straw bed, too. He thought about what she had said about friends, then he looked right at her, "I know where there's some straw, I'll be right back." Off he ran. He picked up all the straw on his bed and carried it to the manger.

When the man returned, the manger was filled with straw.

Oscar felt very good inside. This lady had given him the power to give away his straw. His straw! The one thing he had wanted more than anything else in the whole wide world. He gave it away! He was beginning to learn what Sidney meant about friendship hurting. Somehow, it didn't seem to matter. Joy was bubbling over inside him. She had touched his heart and every part of him. Oscar did not understand how he could give part of himself away and have more. But that's what had happened.

The cry of a newborn baby broke his thinking. He saw a little boy, all pink. The man wrapped him in a big white blanket and laid him in the manger. The baby rested softly on the straw.

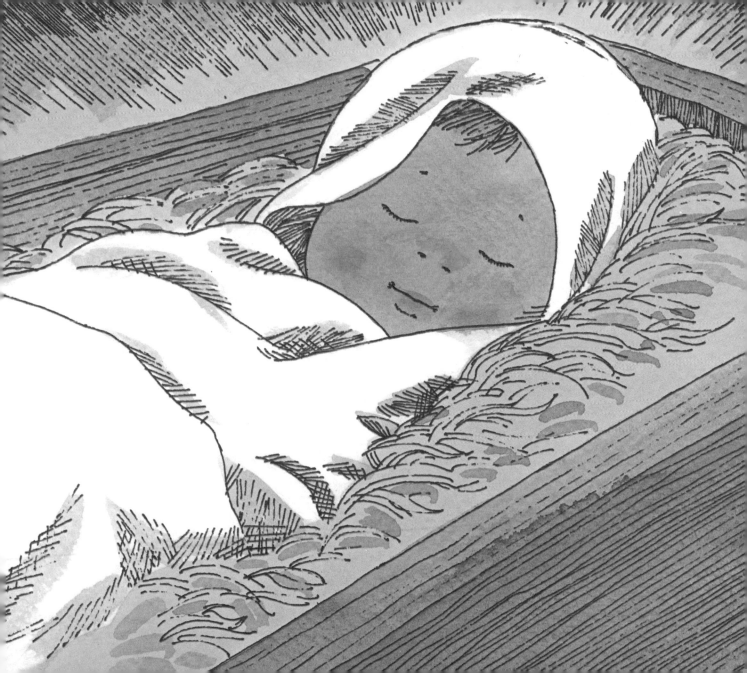

Oscar thought of his own family: Perhaps my father was right. I shall wait until the springtime to have my straw.
With that he left the stable.

His heart was light and his feet seemed to fly over the ground. The sun had just started to come up when Oscar got home. He came in and climbed into his bed. He had just closed his eyes when his father's voice woke him; "Come on, Oscar, wake up! We have a big day today. Come on, sleepy head! Why, you'd think you'd been up all night instead of asleep in your bed!"

"OK, dad; I'm coming," said Oscar, and as he got out of bed he realized that he was smiling.